Easy As Apple Pie

A HARRY AND EMILY ADVENTURE

by Karen Gray Ruelle

Holiday House / New York

For Nina, who likes apples,
and Lee, who doesn't

Printed in the United States of America
www.holidayhouse.com
First Edition

Library of Congress Cataloging-in-Publication Data
Ruelle, Karen Gray.
Easy as apple pie / Karen Gray Ruelle. – 1st ed.
p. cm.
Summary: Emily says "Yuck" whenever apples are mentioned,
but when she and her older brother, Harry, sleep over
at their grandparents' house, they all pick apples
and make them into delicious pies.
ISBN 0-8234-1759-X
[1. Apples–Fiction. 2. Pies–Fiction.
3. Grandparents–Fiction. 4. Sleepovers–Fiction.]
I. Title.
PZ7.R88525 Eas 2002
[E]–dc21
2001059448

Contents

1. Yuck!

At breakfast Harry ate a waffle
with applesauce.
Emily ate a waffle without applesauce.
"I remember when I stayed
with Grandma and Grandpa,"
said Harry.
"We picked apples."

"Yuck," said Emily.

"I don't like apples."

"Everyone likes apples," said Harry.

"Apples are hard and shiny," said Emily.

"Apples might have a worm inside."

She made a face.

"I miss Grandma and Grandpa," said Harry.

"Would you like to visit Grandma and Grandpa next week?" asked their mother.

"Where would we sleep?"
asked Emily.
"You would sleep in my old room,"
said their mother.
"Where would you and Dad sleep?"
asked Harry.
"You and Emily can go without us.

Grandma and Grandpa can spend special time with just you two," said their father.

"I don't want to go unless you go, too," said Emily.

"Oh, Emily, it will be fun," said Harry.
"When I was little, I had fun
at Grandma and Grandpa's house."
"You and Grandpa made me
an apple pie," said their mother.
"It was so good!" said Harry.
"Yuck," said Emily.
"I don't like apple pie."
"How do you know?" asked Harry.
"You have never tried it."
"I would love to eat a homemade
apple pie," said their father.
"Yuck," said Emily.

2. Picking Apples

Harry and Emily waved from
Grandma and Grandpa's car.
"Good-bye!" they said.
"Good-bye!" said their mother
and father. "Have fun!
Don't forget to bring us an apple pie!"
They waved and blew kisses.

Harry looked out the car window.
Emily was too small to see out.
"Are we there yet?" she asked.
"We will be there in two hours,"
said Grandpa.
Grandma turned on the radio.
She found some nice music.
They all sang along.
Halfway there, they stopped for lunch.

"We will have a surprise dessert later,"
said Grandpa.
After lunch, Harry and Emily
fell asleep in the car.
"Wake up, sleepyheads,"
said Grandma. "We are here."
Harry and Emily got out of the car.
They looked around.
There was no house.
There were rows and rows of trees.

"Where is your house?" asked Emily.

"We are at the apple orchard,"
said Grandpa.

"We can pick apples today.
Tomorrow we will make apple pie."

"Hooray!" said Harry.

Emily did not say anything.

"Here is your surprise dessert,"
said Grandpa.
He gave them each a rosy red apple.
Emily frowned.

"No, thank you," she said.

It was fun picking apples,
even if Emily did not eat any.
Harry climbed a tall ladder.

He grabbed an apple and twisted it.
The apple came off the branch.
He took a big juicy bite.

Emily climbed another ladder.
She twisted and twisted an apple.
Finally, the apple came off.
Grandma put it in a basket.

Harry and Emily ran around
under the trees.
Soon the apple basket was full.

"I think we have enough,"
said Grandpa.
He put the basket in the car.
"Don't eat all those apples
before we get home," said Grandma.
"I won't," said Emily.

3. The Midnight Snack

Harry and Emily followed
Grandma upstairs.
Their room was very cozy.
It had yellow walls and yellow curtains
and yellow flowers in a vase.
"I bet you like yellow,"
said Emily to her grandma.

"How did you know!" said Grandma.

She went back downstairs.

Harry and Emily unpacked their bags.

Soon it began to get dark.

Long shadows filled the room.

"It is kind of creepy," said Emily.

"It is not," said Harry.

But he turned on the light anyway.

After dinner, Grandpa said,
"Let's sort the apples.
The big ones are for pies.
The small ones are for snacks."
"What about the ones with worms?"
asked Emily.
Harry and Emily sorted apples.
When they were done,
Harry ate three snack apples.
Emily found other things
to do with them.

That night, Emily could not sleep.

There were creepy shadows.

There were creepy noises.

"Go to sleep," said Harry.

But Emily could not sleep.

Then she noticed a wonderful smell.
It was coming from downstairs.
"What is that yummy smell?" she said.
"It smells like cookies," said Harry.
Emily's tummy started to growl.
"Let's go down and see what that is."
They tiptoed down to the kitchen.

There on the table were two piecrusts.
They were still warm from the oven.
They didn't have any apples in them.
They were empty apple pies.
And they looked yummy.
"Nobody will mind if we try a little,"
said Emily.
She broke off a piece.

It was very hot.

She dropped it on the floor.

"Oh," she said.

Harry blew on the crust to cool it off.

Then he picked off two pieces.

"I like empty apple pie," said Emily.

She broke off another piece and ate it.

"Oh, no," said Harry.

"Now it is uneven."

He broke off a piece
from the other side.
He and Emily split it.
But now the other side was too small.
"We might as well eat this, too,"
he said.
After a few minutes,
the empty apple pie was gone.
"Oh, no," said Harry.
"We have eaten up Grandpa's crust."
Emily tried to push the other
crust to the middle of the table.
It broke in half.
"I guess we better eat this, too."

They jammed the rest of the crust
into their mouths.
Then they ran back upstairs.
"I hope Grandpa doesn't notice,"
Emily said.
Harry and Emily felt bad.
They felt so bad,
they forgot to be scared.
But their tummies were full and happy.
Soon Harry and Emily
were fast asleep.

4. Yum!

"Who wants to make apple pie?"
asked Grandpa the next morning.
Emily pushed her oatmeal around.
Harry stared at his bowl.
"You two are very quiet this morning,"
said Grandma.

Emily's eyes filled with tears.
"Are you homesick?" asked Grandma.
Emily shook her head.
"I know you don't like apples,"
said Grandma.
"But don't be so sad.
Grandpa made a surprise for you.
He made some empty piecrusts
just for you, Emily.

You can fill them
with something else besides apples."
Emily started to cry.
"There are no more crusts,"
said Harry quietly.
"They smelled so good.
We just took a little taste.
Then we took another little taste.
And then, before we knew it,
both crusts were all gone."

Grandpa smiled.

He handed Emily a tissue.

"Did you like my piecrusts?"

Grandpa asked Emily.

She nodded her head.

"They were the best apple pies I have ever eaten," she said with a smile.

"But they would taste even better with apples in them," Harry said.

After breakfast, Harry and Emily
helped Grandpa make another pie.
They filled the crust with apple.
They sprinkled brown sugar
and cinnamon on top.
It was as easy as apple pie.
Grandpa put it in the oven.
The pie smelled so good.
Even Emily tried some.
It was so good,
Harry tried some two or three times.

"It is a good thing we are staying
until tomorrow," said Harry
as he ate the last piece of pie.
"We have to make
another pie for Mom and Dad."
"Next time you come to visit,
we can make peach pie,"
said Grandma.
"That sounds yummy," said Harry.
"Yuck," said Emily.
"I don't like peaches."